W9-BOB-328

Sleep Tight, Little Mouse

2750

MARY MORGAN

Alfred A. Knopf · New York

THIS IS A BORZOI BOOK PUBLISHED BY ALFRED A. KNOPF

Copyright © 2003 by Mary Morgan
All rights reserved under International and Pan-American Copyright
Conventions. Published in the United States by Alfred A. Knopf, an imprint of
Random House Children's Books, a division of Random House, Inc., New York, and
simultaneously in Canada by Random House of Canada Limited, Toronto.
Distributed by Random House, Inc., New York.
KNOPF, BORZOI BOOKS, and the colophon are registered trademarks
of Random House, Inc.

www.randomhouse.com/kids

Library of Congress Cataloging-in-Publication Data
Morgan-Vanroyen, Mary.
Sleep tight, little mouse / written and illustrated by Mary Morgan. — 1st ed.
p. cm.
SUMMARY: At bedtime just before falling asleep, Little Mouse comes to
realize that the best place for him to be is at home with his mother.
ISBN 0-375-82308-5 (trade) — ISBN 0-375-92308-X (lib. bdg.)
[1. Mice—Fiction. 2. Mother and child—Fiction. 3. Bedtime—Fiction.] I. Title.
PZ7.M82535 Sl 2003
[E]—dc21
2002029913

Printed in the United States of America
May 2003
10 9 8 7 6 5 4 3 2
First Edition

For Jean and Jeanine with love, Mary.

Every night Little Mouse slept in his soft, grassy bed.

And every night his mama said, "Good night, my Little Mouse, sleep tight." Then she would smooth his whiskers and kiss his cheek.

But on this night,
Little Mouse was restless.

He tossed and turned
and thought.

"Mama? I wish I could sleep in a nest like a bird."

"Up high in the trees with a
breeze to rock me to sleep."

"And in the morning you can come for breakfast,"
said Little Mouse.

"Yummy," said Mama, "a delicious worm breakfast."

"Oh no! I don't like worms," cried Little Mouse, and he thought and thought some more.

"Mama? I wish I could sleep with a pile of puppies."

"All soft and warm, asleep in a heap."

"When we wake up, you can come for a walk with us,"
said Little Mouse.

"You will look handsome in a collar," said Mama.

"Oh no! I don't like collars," said Little Mouse, and he
thought and thought some more.

"Mama? Maybe I could sleep with some bats in a cave."

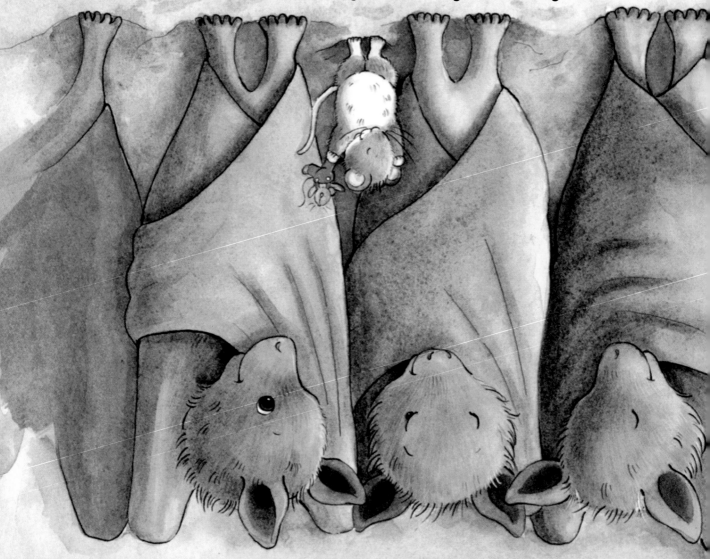

"All stretched out straight from my toes to my nose."

"What fun to hang upside down," said Mama.

"But maybe my toes will get tired," said Little
Mouse. So he thought and thought some more.
"Mama? I wish I could sleep with some otters
on the water."

"I will float like a boat,
rocking on the waves."

"Oh, how lovely," said Mama.
"Yes," sighed Little Mouse.

"But mother otters give their babies baths," said Little Mouse. "I don't like baths." So he thought and thought some more.

"I know. I'll sleep like a joey in a kangaroo's pouch."

"Then wherever we'd roam,
I'd still be at home."

"Yes, yes, Little Mouse!" said Mama. "And you could even snooze while the kangaroos hop, hop, hopped all around."

"No, no. That sounds too bouncy. What if I fall out?"
Little Mouse yawned. His eyes started to close.

"Mama? Maybe I will sleep with a polar bear and her cubs."

"You could snuggle up warm all winter long," said Mama.

"I couldn't stay all winter long, Mama. I would miss you."

Little Mouse closed his eyes. "I am too sleepy to think anymore. I will think of somewhere else to sleep tomorrow."
    Then Mama Mouse tucked him into his very own soft, grassy bed. She smoothed his whiskers and kissed his cheek.

"Good night, my Little Mouse.
Sleep tight," she said.
But he was already fast asleep.